Skippyjon Jones

CLASS ACTION

JUDY SCHACHNER

SCHOLASTIC INC.
New York Toronto London Auckland
Sydney Mexico City New Delhi Hong Kong

To Nora Kate O'Sullivan, a true Spanish lass—
Love, Judy

My gratitude to all of Team Skippy
and thanks to Cha Cha, the bigges
of the small ones in the mirror
and in memory of Mitzi Ambrose

ISBN 978-0-545-39202-

Copyright © 2011 by Judith Byron Schachner. All rights reserved
Published by Scholastic Inc., 557 Broadway, New York, NY 10012, b
arrangement with Dutton Children's Books, a division of Penguin Youn
Readers Group, a member of Penguin Group (USA) Inc. SCHOLASTIC an
associated logos are trademarks and/or registered trademarks of Scholastic Inc

12 11 10 9 8 7 6 5 4 3 2 1   11 12 13 14 15 16/

Printed in Mexico   4

First Scholastic printing, September 201

Designed by Heather Woo

The illustrations for this book were created in acrylics an
pen and ink on Aquarelle Arches watercolor pape

Skippyjon Jones was just dying to go to school.

And nobody, not even his mama, was going to stop him. But she did, by the scruff of his neck.

"School is for the DOGS!" stated Mama Junebug Jones emphatically.

"They're **unruly** and **drooly**," she added dramatically.

"Just *listen* to that barking— those hounds sound **ferocious**."

"Plus a bus full of dog breath would smell so **atrocious**.

Good golly, pop lollie! It's such a **no-brainer**.

If there is a good dog, it's because of its *trainer*."

His mama gently nudged her nugget into his room.

Then she added, "You're Skippyjon Jones, a smart Siamese cat. Take a look in the mirror if you don't believe that."

"He looks in the mirror every day," said his sisters, Jezebel, Jilly Boo, and Ju-Ju Bee, "but all he sees are Chi-wa-las."

"*Arff, arff,*" barked Ju-Ju Bee.

After his family left him to think, the Chi-wa-la did exactly what his mama suggested.

But not before he bounced around his room with some books.

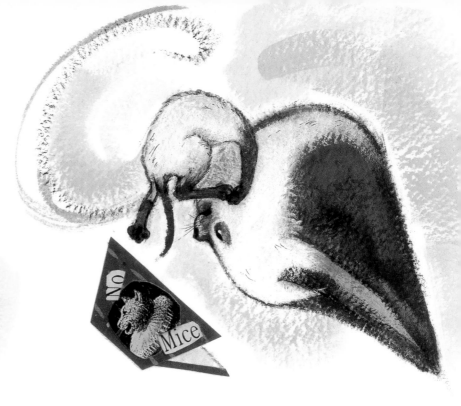

"Oh, I'm *Skippyjonjones,*

And I don't get the fuss.

"It's not like a pigeon

Is driving the bus."

Then he climbed up his sisters' kitty-condo
ladder for a peekaboo in the mirror.

"**Holy Julio!**" squealed the kitty boy.

"How many Chihuahuas am I?" he wondered out loud.

Then he took a deep breath and, using his very best Spanish accent, he answered, "As many as your head can handle, *hombre*."

And quicker than you can say "the cat in the hat never did that," the kitty boy tossed his mask and his cape and a bright yellow banana into his *mochila*. Then, as he buttoned up his red plaid shirt, he began to sing in a *muy, muy* soft voice.

"Oh, my name is Skippito Friskito, (clap-clap)

And I'm off to the school for perritos, (clap-clap)

'Cuz I've got a good hunch

That I'm going to have lunch

With a grande ol' bunch of poochitos." (clap-clap)

Just across the hall, Mama Junebug Jones and the girls were doing a little homework of their own.

"Listen here, Messy Missies," said Mama, "how are you supposed to clean your kitty condo without your ladder?"

"Skippyjon has it," said the sisters.

"What for?" asked Mama.

"So he can see the Chi-wa-la in the mirror."

The Chi-wa-la, however, was already in his closet, boarding a bus for school.

Blocks

BUS STOP

But the kitty boy wasn't the only Chihuahua on board. His old *amigos*, Los Chimichangos, were going to school, too.

"Thank dog you made it, dude!" exclaimed Don Diego, the biggest of the small ones.

BARKER ☖ ACADEMY

"*Si*, Skippito," panted Poquito Tito, the smallest of the small ones. "We need your help *con el* bull-ito."

"Without a doubt-ito," declared El Skippito. "But why do you need my help with the bully?"

"Because he is a *perro mezquino*," declared Don Diego, "who *barrenas* around the *escuela* in a *tazalita*."

"He spins around the school in a **tiny teacup?**" exclaimed the kitty boy in shock.

"*Sí*, dude," added Don Diego. "He growls and howls and wears a *suérte de lana también*."

"Not the WOOL sweater," said Skippito.

"Uh-huh," agreed Poquito Tito, trembling. "He is a woolly bully."

There wasn't a dog worth his biscuits who didn't fear the woolly bully, so it wasn't a surprise when a potent puff of panic poofed out the *gatito*'s tail.

And all that puffiness inspired the poochitos to sing:

"Oh, Puff-ee, Puff-oo, Puff-ito,
(clap-clap)
We know you can do it, Skippito.
(clap-clap)
Let's unravel his sweater
And knit something better.
We'll show that old woolly bull-ito."
(clap-clap)

But there was no turning back now.
The doggies had arrived at school.

A moment later, the principal,
a poodle with very high standards,
appeared with a bucket of balls
and a whistle.

First she BLEW.

And then she
THREW!

"Go fetch!"
barked Mrs. Begalot.

Then every dog, big and small, chased a ball
down the hall and into their classrooms.
Except for Skippito. He got carried along by
the river of rovers and . . .

. . . landed in art class where he drew his best ever double doggie doodle.

"I've never seen a pup do that before," said Mrs. Houndler, the art teacher.

THE HOWL

THE MONA FLEASA

Then he trotted over to the music room and bayed like a beagle for the canine chorus.

"Bow-*WOW!*" woofed Mr. Muzzletuff. "What a pair of ears."

After music came math, where Skippy stunned Mrs. McDrooler with his counting skills.

"Two . . . three . . . five . . . seven . . . eleven."

Chabina

1
+1
2

Poquito

300
+20
50

Ickky

2
+2
4

Snub.

5
+5
10

At the bell, the *amigos* followed their noses into the library.
Not even a bowl full of *frijoles* smelled as delicious as the scent of
books waiting to be read.

"I lick *libros*!" declared El Skippito Friskito, the great reader-ito.
"I like books, too," whispered Leonora Lappsitter, the librarian,
from behind the bookcase.

The kitty boy was the last to leave the library, so he had to race right over to French class with Monsieur Foozay.

"Can you say *cheese*?" asked the teacher.

"*Oui, oui!*" said zee poodles. "*Fromage.*"

"*Sí, sí,*" said Skippito. "*¡Queso!*"

"*¡Queso Cabeza!*" shouted the Chimichangos from the rear of the room.

"I'm not a cheese head, Chimichangos!" chuckled the *gatito*. "I'm a Chihuahua!"

The poodles were tickled pink to have *los* poochitos in class with them. And *los* poochitos wanted to share what they had learned with their *amigo*.

Zo zee poopies zang:

"Comme-çi, Comme-ça, Comme-cito (clap-clap)

we have zumzing to tell you, Skippito.

When zee poodles say Oui, (clap-clap)

zay really mean Sí,

So don't look for a red hydrant-ito!"

(clap-clap)

After French, *los muchachos* took a pass on Obedience Class, deciding instead to nap inside the warm case with the golden *trofeos*.

"I'm not good at following rules," confessed the kitty boy.

"What dog *IS*, dude?" quipped Don Diego.

But just then, the *gatito* heard a gut-gurgling growl that shook the entire *escuela*, perhaps the whole *planeta*.

"Holy heartburn!" hollered Skippito. "Was that my tummy?"

"No. That is the bellow of the woolly bull-ito," said Poquito Tito with a shiver-ito.

The gruesome grumble grew
louder, and along with it came the
rattle and plink of the terrible *tazalita*.
It was spinning wildly, right under his nose,
circling like a polka-dotted shark.

"*¡Andele!*" declared Don Diego. "Get out your duds, dude."
But Skippito was too frozen with fear to unpack his *mochila*. So his
amigos did it for him, helping to change their *chico* into El Skippito
Friskito, complete with mask, cape, and banana.

"Why the *plátano*, dude?" asked Pinto Lito.
"It's my snack-ito," replied the *gatito*.
"Will you share it with me and Tito?"
"Yes, indeed-o," agreed Skippito.

Then *woof* *chuck-a-luck-a-luck-a,* *woof* *chuck-a-luck-a-luck-a,* every doggie leaped out of the case and latched onto the turbo-charged *taza*.

This caused the cup to spin wildly out of control, some of the *chicos* just hanging on by a tail.

"Estoy mareado," cried Skippito.

"You are not dizzy, dude, you're **green**," yipped the doggies.

The whirling dervish of a dog-filled teacup cut a mean path of destruction past the principal's office and spun straight on into the lunch bunch like a bowling ball.

"Strike-ito!" shouted the poochitos.

And strike it did.
Smash! Crackle! and Pop!

The twirling *tazalita* crashed right into a table and broke apart, exposing the fur-rocious fuzzy for what he really was—a teeny-tiny, itsy-bitsy, wool-wearing teacup Chihuahua.

"Dude!" declared Skippito. "You're no bigger than a bug-ito!"

But the bug-ito's only reply was a gut-gurgling growl greater than the hounds had ever heard before.

"Is that your tummy?" asked Skippito.

"*Sí*," replied the bull-ito. "*Tengo mucho hambre.*"

"I am hungry, too," agreed the *gatito*, "but you can have my *plátano*."

This act of kindness made the Chimichangos pull
out their jump rope right in the middle of the mess.

Peanut butter and belly buttons,

Chunky cherry pits,

The woolly bully's taza

Has broken into bits!

Wiggle-waggle, wiggle-waggle,

Jelly on the toast,

He's not a woolly bully.

He's just hungrier than most!

Just then, Mrs. Begalot stomped into the lunchroom.
"I smell a cat!" she bellowed. "That cat better scat!"

Then out came the whistle.

First she BLEW,
and then she *THREW*
a bright yellow ball down the hall, which
every dog, big and small, began to chase.
Except for Skippito. He wasn't chasing
the ball. He was running for his life.

First Skippy TRIPPED,
and then he *SLIPPED*
on the banana peel and slid straight out of
his closet . . .

. . . and back into the arms of his Mama Junebug Jones.

"What in the woolly white willies have you been up to, Mr. Whistle Whiskers?" asked Mama.

"He broke my teacup," whined Jilly Boo.

"And he ate my banana," complained Jezebel.

"That's 'cuz he went to school with the Chi-wa-las," explained Ju-Ju Bee.

Later that night, after every fuzzy fell asleep,
the kitty boy was good for one last bounce.

"Oh, I'm Skippyjonjones,

And I couldn't say it better,

A dog is not a bully

Just because he wears a sweater!"

Then he bounced over to his mama and gave her a *beso*,
a kiss she felt straight through the layers of her quilt.
"Good night, Little Dipper," said the very sleepy mama.
"G'night, Mama," said the very sleepy kitten.